VENUS NEXT DOOR

EXTENDED VERSION

NICCOYAN ZHENG

DISCLAIMER:

Venus Next Door Extended Version © 2024 by Niccoyan Zheng

ISBN: 978-1-7390363-5-5

ISBN Paperback: 978-1-998359-13-4

Editing by: Editor: All That's Wright & Edits Done Wright

Cover Design by: SIP (Swirl Interracial Publications)

Formatting: SIP (Swirl Interracial Publications)

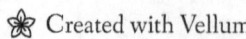 Created with Vellum

This book is dedicated to the sister authors, who have encouraged me and cheered me on at every step.

Venus Next Door

DISCLAIMER:

AUTHOUR NOTE:

Things to beware of in this book: adult language, and graphic sexual content.

🍁 Side note, I am Canadian, and as the majority of the story is in Canada. The spelling and word usage contained in the story are also Canadian. 🍁

PLAYLIST

Music is at the heart of my writing process.

Here are some songs that spoke to me with this book:

- I'll Make Love To You by Boys II Men
- Irreplaceable by Beyonce
- Lady in Red by Chris de Burgh
- Let's Give Them Something to Talk by Bonnie Raitt
- Take a bow by Rhianna
- Truly Madly Deeply by Savage Garden

AUTHOUR'S NOTE:

Things to beware of in this book: adult language, and graphic sexual content.

✻ Side note, I am Canadian, and the story's location is in Canada. So, the spelling and word usage contained in the story are also Canadian. ✻

"You come to love not by finding the perfect person, but by seeing an imperfect person perfectly."

SAM KEEN

NOT INTERESTED IN YOUR COOKIES

VEE

Isaac Lam cannot stand me. He's my next-door neighbour, and he took an instant dislike to me from the moment I moved into our quiet cul-de-sac.

It was two days before Valentine's Day, and Vee was outside putting on the final touches to her holiday décor. The cul-de-sac in the quiet city on the outskirts of Toronto was cold, quiet, and dark. The sun had already set, and all the other residents were nestled away in their homes. However, there was no other place Vee would rather be. It was her love of all things holiday, which drove her to celebrate them in an overblown fashion. Vee did have favourites and Valentine's Day was in her top four.

Every year, she selected a theme. This year it was Gnomes. Stepping back, she admired the door cover filled with Gnomes surrounded by and holding hearts. Seeing that it was her inaugural

V-day as a first-time homeowner, she was going all out. Gnomes in all shades of red and pink lined her walkway and the porch.

Vee next set her sight on the task of setting up the inflatables. The cute four-foot cupid Gnome holding his arrow went up without issue. However, the green frog with the Gnome cap that was holding a heart that read 'Be My Valentine', had her struggling to get it to inflate. Of course, the moment she won her battle with the five-foot amphibian, and it stood in all its Valentine's Day glory, was the same moment Mr. Cheerful selected to come home. He backed his humongous truck into the driveway and sat there scowling at her. She could feel his disdain from across the street. The cab lights were on, so once he shut off the headlights the annoyance on his very handsome face became visible.

It wasn't the first time she thought about how truly beautiful the man would be if he would stop all that glowering. Vee had the same thought, at their initial encounter. She had spent the first day in her new home, baking a welcome gift for her new neighbours. Taking her time, she had assembled a beautiful basket with cookies, brownies, blondies, and added bags of her own tea blend.

The street had five houses. Vee's house was the first as you entered the end of the street. Most of her neighbours were either retired or close to it. So, it had taken Vee completely by surprise to find that the occupant of the last house was a tall Asian man who looked to be in his late thirties. She had openly stared at him in shock.

Her gaze swept his six-foot beefy frame, from head to toe. He looked like a walking poster for the army, due to his buzz cut, and t-shirt stretched over his massive pecs. His biceps tested the molecular strength of the fabric. He'd even managed to get the tree trunks posing as legs into green cargo pants. In all of her days she had never seen a beard that perfectly groomed. It was full, and thick, surrounding a thinner upper lip accompanied by a fuller bottom. His chocolate brown eyes were intense.

"Yes, can I help you?" He gruffly inquired.

"Oh yes, sorry, I'm new to the cul-de-sac. I just moved in the house across the street. I stopped by to introduce myself. My name is Vee Desmond, and this is for you," she added, holding out the basket.

Giving it a cursory glance, he'd dismissed her offerings, grumbling, "no thanks, not interested." He folded his arms and gave her a hard, icy stare. Okay, this wasn't what she was expecting.

"I'm not selling anything. This is a gift." Vee had brightly supplied. He must have misunderstood. Who said no to a gift? Especially one made with such care. The basket was wrapped in clear cellophane, topped off with a navy-blue bow.

"Look Lady, I'm not interested in your cookies, or whatever else you have in that basket." With that declaration he'd promptly closed the door in her face. The whole incident had hurt her feelings. She often used gifts to break the ice. No one had ever reacted in that manner before. For the life of her, she couldn't figure out why they had gotten off on the wrong foot.

Since then, every attempt she had made to get on his good side was dismissed or shot down. If she waved in his direction, he just stared back. If she came outside while he was out, then he would retreat inside. She even left him some treats on his doorstep. He returned them, leaving them on her porch. Vee couldn't get near him to try to repair the fallout of their initial meeting.

Hell, the only reason she even knew his name was Isaac was because their neighbours had supplied her with it. While he was gruff, and she had never seen him smile, his scowl disappeared in the presence of others. Then he would look at her and it would magically reappear. Isaac didn't seem to have a problem with anyone else in their little community. Mrs. Emerson had even called him 'a sweet boy'.

After remaining in his vehicle for a few minutes, Isaac shut off his truck and got out. His eyes remained fixed in her direction as he slammed his door.

"Jianke," he called out.

How did Vee forget about Isaac's big ragdoll cat that sat on her porch? Jianke stretched lazily, taking his time before he strolled off her property, back across the street to his home. Once he reached his yard, the feline rubbed against his owner's legs and was promptly picked up.

"Hello Isaac." She called out, waving at him. He didn't wave back, but he nodded in her direction. Progress. Very little, but she would take it. It was the most she had made since she moved in, in June. He turned to walk away, then halted.

"Hey Lady, stop feeding my cat," he demanded.

"I don't feed him. I think he just likes visiting me."

Isaac didn't bother to answer her, he just scoffed at her. Great, another reason for him to dislike her. He had gotten the cat a few months ago and the feline liked to divide his time between the two properties.

Maybe Jianke liked it over at her house because it was warm and inviting. Vee worked hard to recreate the warmth that her mom had provided her before she had turned nine. Soon after MS had come into their lives, robbing her mom of her vitality. Her parents made the decision to give up their beautiful two-story home for an apartment that could accommodate her mom's mobility issues.

Once they moved, her mom didn't have the physical strength or cheer to decorate for the holidays like she used to. They no longer had celebrations to make their house a home. The holidays became like any other day. Those were sad times.

Vee woke up one morning after waiting on a boyfriend who wasn't ready to take the next step after five years and decided she would no longer sit around waiting. She broke things off with Dylan. She took control of her own life and made her own decisions. Taking her savings, she bought a home that reminded her of her childhood. Vee set about to keep her mother's spirit alive. Looking around at her Valentine's Day décor she smiled, knowing her mom would have loved this.

2

FULL BOOBS AND BOBBY SOCKS

ISAAC

Vee is so stinking cheerful. All the time. It wears on my nerves. There is no reason for anyone to be that cheerful all the time. None!

Isaac Lam decided to live in the house his grandmother left him because her neighbours were quiet and kept to themselves. He loved coming and going without having to engage in small talk with fellow residents on his street. They had known him since he was a kid and accepted that the most they would get out of him was a nod and quick wave.

The bonus was that they were elderly and no longer engaged in decorating their homes to signal the arrival of holidays. Isaac was decidedly not festive and appreciated that his neighbours didn't allow their holiday cheer to spill out to the exterior of their homes. They kept it indoors where he wasn't forced to encounter it every time he came home.

It had been a good run. He lived in suburban bliss for five years. Until last June 1st, when the newest addition to the street moved in. Isaac hadn't been prepared. He didn't know the elderly gentleman across the way had even put his house up for sale. There was a moving truck moving him out one day, and hours later there was another moving the new owner in. He hadn't gotten a look at them because well he didn't really care. He'd gone about his day, not giving it another thought.

That was until his new neighbour came to introduce herself. When he'd opened the door, he was not expecting the attractive russet-skinned woman on his doorstep. He had discreetly given an appreciative appraisal of her five-foot five-inch curvy frame. From the top of her head, with its carefree dark curls threaded with caramel highlights, parted into two perfect pigtails, to her full bust covered up by a pink t-shirt underneath dark denim overall shorts, all the way to her sneakers with bobby socks. Also, very pink. Her topaz-coloured eyes were filled to the brim with warmth. It immediately reminded him of those frigging Care Bears. The woman on his porch had a smile that was carefree and bright. Her face was an open book and was not as discreet with its own appraisal. For a moment he was happy with the unexpected pleasure of a beautiful woman on his doorstep. That was until he put two and two together and figured out that she must be his new neighbour.

The realization bothered him to no end. That meant she was off limits. Which was a damned shame. He had a laundry list of ideas to change the cheerful expression to one of pleasure-laced delight.

When he told her, "no thanks, not interested." That message was for her in regard to the basket and for himself concerning her.

Could he have been more pleasant to her? Probably. However, he knew her type. She would take it as a sign to befriend him. An idea to which he was very opposed. So, he nipped any neighbourly friendliness in the bud.

Women like her, full of light, would profess they would be able to handle your darkness. However, in the end they would walk away, leaving you broken-hearted. Isaac knew firsthand, his ex-wife was one of those women. Nancy couldn't handle the danger of being married to a cop, so he walked away from the force for her. It wasn't enough. She wasn't able to hang while he built his landscaping company. So, even after his sacrificing his job for a new one, Nancy had taken all that sunshine and left him anyway.

Isaac was content with one night stands far away from his home. He had to be because, although Vee was everywhere and spoken about by everyone, she was off limits.

Mrs. Emerson had other ideas. The older woman had an agenda. One day after he'd pruned her bushes, she had insisted he come in for some lemonade and Bacon Chocolate Chip Cheesecake bars. He'd thanked her for her delicious snack. Only to have Mrs. Emerson inform him, "It isn't me you should be thanking. Vee made them. Actually, be a dear and return the container to her. Oh, maybe ask her for some more. I'm sure she would be happy to share." The container never made it back over to Vee, his personal assignment was to avoid her.

It wouldn't be the first time he would be pushed in her direction. "Be a dear and help Vee set up for the block party."

A BBQ block party that Isaac thought was the embodiment of hell. Who celebrated Civic Day? No one! It was a nice day off in the middle of summer. All his neighbours outside milling around, sharing meals, socializing, and listening to music. That had been just the beginning. He watched as Vee's cheer infected his street.

Halloween had truly been the beginning of the end... for the first time since he moved in, he saw children invade the cul-de-sac. By Christmas, most of the other houses were decorated in their community.

Now it was the Valentine's season and Vee had converted the rest of the cul-de-sac. Isaac couldn't escape the day. Although he desperately wanted to forget that he shared his birthday with Valentine's Day. Which was also the day his ex-wife served him with divorce papers. Thankfully, Mother Nature was showing him a little mercy by blanketing all their décor with fresh snow. The bonus was that it would make for a busy day for him and his crew.

Although it was just before four o'clock in the morning and he was barely awake, Isaac started planning out his day. How he and his staff would manage their various clients. He had already decided that he would take care of his neighbours last. They hardly went anywhere. Well, except for Vee, who had not signed up for Lam Landscaping and Snow Removal's services.

Sure, she had the landscaping covered, he was actually impressed at how she cared for her lawn and shrubs. The snow removal is where he knew she would run into trouble. The snowblower she purchased was holding up, but it wouldn't get her through a big snowfall.

3

PLOWING YOUR DRIVEWAY

VEE

Disappointment washed over Vee, looking outside when she woke up. Normally she loved snowy days, but today the blanket of white fluff had covered her beautiful decorations. What was worse, the meteorologists were promising a lot more snow. So much more that it was threatening her evening festivities.

Vee had planned the perfect Valentine's Day soiree. A few friends were supposed to stop by. She had tons of food, drinks, and had baked up a storm. Vee had also managed to find the perfect red dress and matching shoes. Her outfit was sultry and stunning. Damnit, she wanted to wear it! It had been forever since she had dressed up. The outfit screamed grown up sexy woman.

Her daily attire consisted of blue or black suits with neutral colour tops. While her off hours bubbly attire often had her mistaken for a teen.

The day turned out to be short. Her boss had sent them home early because of how heavy the snow was coming down. As Vee navigated her way home, a ride that took her three times as long, her phone kept dinging. On her return home, she was able to check those messages. She wasn't able to pull into her snow-covered driveway.

Although she understood, disappointment washed over her as she read message after message of cancellations. The majority of her friends lived downtown and didn't want to risk the drive out to her house in the inclement weather. As if that wasn't bad enough, now she had to deal with all this snow. She bemoaned her decision to save money by not hiring a snow remover. Money hadn't been her only motivation. Vee hoped the extra activities would help her shed some unwanted pounds. Now she was going to really burn those calories.

After struggling up her driveway through the heavy snow, she went inside and changed into her sweats. Vee kicked herself that she hadn't left her snowblower out, because she then had to shovel a path to her garage. It was made worse by the still, falling heavy, flakes.

It was all going so well. Vee had a quarter of the driveway done when the snowblower stopped. Just died on her. It was then that she took notice of her neighbours' driveways. Isaac was at Ms. Emerson's, and another man wearing the same logo was next door. Their industrial blowers quickly cleared the snow.

Her back was aching, but she tried to keep it upbeat as she listened to tunes and worked to clear the offensive white matter. Maybe she should just do enough to get her car in the driveway. She would deal with everything else tomorrow. Or maybe she could call around and hire someone to do it. Part of her wished she could just walk over to Isaac and hire him on the spot. However, she didn't think it was a good idea to employ her grumpy neighbour, who would probably say no just to spite her. So, she carried on. Until a tap on her shoulder had her shrieking for her life.

Her heart slowed down as she realised it was Isaac.

"You've been out here a while, need some help?" He asked. Vee couldn't recall ever hearing of a Valentine's Day miracle. Yet here she was experiencing one. Isaac was offering to help her. There was no way she would turn it down, she was tired of all this snow. The sooner she could be out of it the better.

"Yes please, my snow blower conked out on me."

"I saw that. Listen, run inside and warm up. I'll have this done in no time."

The words slipped out unbidden, "I can stay out and help." Why Vee had said that she didn't know. She was freezing and wet.

"Its alright, you look like a popsicle. What you can do is give me your keys and I'll move your car in the driveway when I'm done."

"Really?"

"Yeah, it will help me finish up the sidewalk."

"Are you sure?" Vee pressed.

"Yes, I wouldn't feel right about heading inside when you are still out here struggling. Decent job, given you only had a shovel though." Isaac mused.

What the hell was going on? Vee thought. This couldn't be the same man that had been scowling at her for the last eight months.

Whatever was going on, she wasn't about to look a gift horse in the mouth. She gave him her keys and high tailed it into her house.

It was nice to be tucked away in her cozy kitchen, away from all the snow. As she sipped her tea, she looked over all of her preparations for the night. She'd gone overboard on the desserts because of her sweet tooth. Heart shaped cookies, and the decadent red velvet three-layer cake lined her counter. Her fridge had the long-stemmed chocolate covered strawberries and a strawberry cheesecake. Not to mention all the items for the massive heart-shaped charcuterie board.

Her phone rang pulling her from her thoughts.

"Hello, Dear," Mrs. Emerson greeted.

"Hello, Mrs. Emerson."

"Is that Isaac Lam I see over there plowing your driveway?" The question was innocently asked, yet Vee found herself choking on her tea.

"Yes, he came over and offered to help me."

"See, such a sweet boy. Well, if you see him when he is done. You tell him to stop by I have a birthday card for him."

"It's his birthday?"

"Yes see, the sweet boy was born on Valentine's Day. Although his ex-wife tried to forever ruin it for him. Can you imagine serving someone with divorce papers on their birthday? I met her a few times and I never really took to her." Mrs. Emerson tsked. "Anyway, send him my way."

"Would you and Mr. Emerson like to come over for dinner? I was planning a Valentines celebration, but no one can make it."

"Oh, thank you for the offer, Dear, but we've already had an early dinner. Maybe you should extend that offer to Isaac. Bye-bye."

4

GOOD DEED

ISAAC

It had been a long busy day, but it had been exactly what Isaac needed. By the time he and Jimmy had taken care of the residents on his street, he was ready to get inside, take a long shower and grab something to eat. Of course, he could have minded his own business and gone in, but he couldn't in good conscious go into his home and leave Vee out there struggling with the shovel. He had to say he admired her tenacity. Her form was shit, but she was slowly making progress.

Helping her was his good deed of the day. Besides, it wasn't a hardship with his equipment. As he made quick work of the snow removal from her driveway and walkway. He backed her car into her driveway, then did her sidewalk. Just as he finished, she appeared with a mug. He took in her appearance and was glad to see she no longer looked like a popsicle.

"I can't believe you got this done so quickly," Vee praised.

"The equipment helps."

"Yeah, for sure. Here. I made you some hot chocolate. It isn't very sweet but its good."

Isaac briefly thought about not taking the mug, but he appreciated the gesture.

"Thank you for coming to my aid. This would have taken me forever. I really appreciate it since you have better things to do today, especially since it's your birthday and all."

The mention of his birthday erased all the goodwill. First, how did she know. Secondly, he would have preferred to go the whole day without mention of it.

"Yeah, here are your keys," he snapped as he practically flung them at her.

"Thank you again. What do I owe you?"

"Nothing. We are good," he said as he walked away.

"Isaac, I almost forgot Ms. Emerson asked me to tell you to drop by for your card." Oh, that's how she knew. What was the old lady up to? She normally slipped him his birthday card when she paid for her monthly services.

"Yeah, thanks."

"Umm did you have any plans for tonight?" Isaac could tell she was nervous to ask. Vee wasn't making eye contact like she normally did. Instead, she shuffled from one foot to another.

"No, I'm looking forward to getting inside and relaxing for the night."

"Or since you won't take payment for helping me. Umm... you can come over and we could umm... share a meal. Just to say thank you."

"No. Thank you is enough. Good night." Isaac strolled off trying to dismiss the way disappointment and hurt took over Vee's face.

Rather than heading straight home, he detoured to Mrs. Emerson. He had to wait a moment for the elderly lady to come to the door.

"Isaac! You got my message. Here is your card dear," she beamed.

"Thank you for this," he said holding up the card.

"That was wonderful of you to help Vee."

"It was nothing. Well, I'm off. I need to get home."

"Oh my, is it still snowing out there?" She inquired, trying to look beyond him to the outside.

"Yes, although it's slowed down some."

"Ohh, that's good. I was worried about the weather. I am going to try to head over to Vee's. That poor girl planned a get together tonight but it's been snowed out.

Now she is sitting over there all alone with all that food. She is such a good little cook too.

Oh, do you feel that the wind is picking up? I don't know if I can go over there. I just feel horrible. If only someone would go over there and keep her company." Mrs. Emerson was putting her previous acting skills to use. She had acted in the theatre and was calling upon those talents to work his empathy. Well Isaac wasn't falling for it. He was going home and staying there for the night.

"Well, you have a good night, dear," she added, as she patted his cheek.

"You too, Mrs. Emerson." She gave him a look of disappointment as she closed the door.

As he walked through his front door, hunger hit him hard. The long shower he planned would have to be changed to a quick one. He took the frozen chili out of the freezer before he headed off to the washroom. He returned to find Jianke, sitting at the front door meowing to be let out.

"Listen Buddy, it is really crappy out there. You don't want to go out in all that snow."

In response, Jianke scratched at the door, as his meowing became louder.

"Alright, I don't know what you want out there, but I will let you out."

The moment he opened the door, the little traitor bolted from the warmth of his home and sauntered across the street. Great. Well, if Jianke wanted to go visit the neighbour, he was free to.

Isaac headed back to the kitchen and looked at his frozen chili. It had lost all its appeal. Takeout was going to take too long in this weather. He should be a good cat dad and go across the street and get Jianke.

A few minutes later, he was on Vee's doorstep. As she opened the door, two things struck Isaac. One was the warm delicious scents that greeted him. It smelled like a bakery had met a bistro. The scents made his mouth water.

Or maybe it was the second thing that caused the watering. Isaac had seen her many times over the last eight months, but he had never seen her look like this. Her hair was piled up in a bun, displaying her long neck. The dress, yeah, that should be illegal. It dipped low displaying her full mounds, while it molded to every one of her sinful curves stopping right above her knees. Her legs were long and shapely. Lord, they would feel good wrapped around his waist.

"Hey, I guess you are here for your cat?" She asked, pulling him from his wayward thoughts.

"Um yeah."

On cue, Jianke made his way to the front door. Vee turned to pick up the feline. The dress was far more lethal from the back. It dipped low, exposing a large expanse of skin that looked velvety soft. Just as she had the cat in hand, he jumped out of her arms and took off.

"Sorry about that. You can come in. I'll go get him for you."

Isaac stepped inside and closed the door. "Hey before you go off, I'm sorry about earlier. I shouldn't have snapped at you. I'm not big on birthdays."

"Oh, I'm sorry." Worrying her bottom lip, she looked a bit sad. It was unsettling to see the normally cheerful woman looking anything but joyful. It was worse knowing he caused it.

"No need to apologise." he offered. His voice still sounded gruff to his own ears. He tried again.

"You look festive. That dress is umm..."

"Too much?" she offered.

Isaac allowed his gaze to rake over her frame as he answered, "no not at all. I was going to say stunning."

Actually, he was going to say sexy as hell, but he thought based on all their previous exchanges, that may be too much.

5

MONSIEUR CHAT

VEE

Vee recognised an appreciative glance when she saw one. Now she was glad that she decided to wear her dress, although she would spend Valentine's Day alone.

"Thank you," she answered, as she felt the warmth take over her cheeks.

"Since you are here, would you like a drink?" Although she had extended the invitation, she didn't expect it to be accepted. However, that's exactly what he did, as he unzipped his coat. He wore a burgundy sweater that was fitted to his torso and black jeans. It was fair to say she also appreciated his attire.

"Yes, I'd like that. Lead the way," he instructed. She headed to the kitchen with him in tow.

Vee motioned to the bar stool at the counter, and Isaac removed his coat placed it on the back of the chair and had a seat.

"I have wine. Rosé or white. Beer, Labatt Blue. For pop I have Ginger Ale and Pepsi. What is your pleasure?" She offered.

"I'll take a Blue. Man, it smells good in here."

"Well, since you're having a drink, would you like to stay for something to eat? I've got pot pie in the oven, and tons of hors d'oeuvres in the fridge."

Issac gaze held hers, then accepted her offer. "I'd like that."

"Oh alright." Vee was surprised that Isaac had accepted.

Their hands brushed as she handed him his beer. It sent a little jolt along her spine, and they held each other's gaze.

"Let me get some snacks out." Vee went about setting up a mini charcuterie board as she confirmed his preferences.

"Honestly, I am not a picky eater, I'll enjoy whatever you serve." He smiled and shrugged. It was a good thing that man went through life keeping that smile hidden. It was positively sinful. He had perfect straight white teeth. It threw her off for a moment.

Once she assembled the board, she placed it on the counter and grabbed herself a beer as well.

"I can put on the television or music if you prefer."

"I don't watch much TV unless it is sports, so music will be fine." After some back and forth, Isaac insisted that she play whatever she wanted. For a Grumpy Gus, he was surprisingly easygoing. *Maybe it was because he was being fed?* The man could pack it away. Which was understandable, as he had all that muscle to sustain.

Vee was actually having a good time, and she was enjoying surprising him.

"This is a good selection of tunes," he praised after the second song. "The truth be told, I was expecting sappy ballads, not Canadian Rock. What?" He paused as Vee shrugged and wrinkled her nose.

"Did I speak too soon?" Isaac inquired.

"No, I was messing with you. Just because I love being festive doesn't mean I listen to sentimental music."

They ate and talked about what turned out to be their mutual love of rock. Two beers later, he looked around her kitchen and asked, "so what's with all the decorations? It looks like cupid barfed all over your place."

"Umm wow, rude much? If you must know, it makes me feel closer to my Mom. She loved all this stuff. So, yeah, I might be over the top, but I'm keeping her memories alive."

"Sorry for your loss. Well, no one can say you are half-assing it." Isaac reached over and squeezed her hand. Again, it ignited that zip she felt earlier. His hand lingered as he drew closer to her.

The sound of meowing drew their attention as Jianke made an appearance.

"Oh, can I give him a snack? I think he's hungry." Vee sounded concerned.

"Give him what you usually do."

"I told you I don't feed your cat. Monsieur Chat just likes hanging out with me."

"Wait? Did you rename my cat?" Isaac laughed.

"Well, at first, I didn't know his name, so that's what I called him. Can I give him some tuna?"

"Sure. So, you charmed my cat without the aid of food?"

"Of course, I'm really charming," she replied sassily.

Vee had Jianke fed in short order. As soon as he was finished, the cat sauntered out of the kitchen. They watched as he made himself at home curling his feline body into her armchair.

"Are you a vet?" Isaac inquired

"No, why would you ask that?"

"With all that sunshine, I figured you did something that made people happy. Guessed that's why Jianke was drawn to you."

Vee couldn't help the laughter that bubbled out of her.

"No. Very far from it. I spend my day crunching numbers. I'm an auditor."

"Don't tell me you're with the Canadian Revenue Agency."

"I used to be until a year ago." Vee went on to explain it was hard on her psyche the vitriol that she often received because of her job.

"So where do you work now?"

"I work for Ma's Kitchen." Vee replied.

"The company that celebrity Chef Aaron Ma owns?"

"If he heard you call him a celebrity chef, he would lose it."

"So, what's it like working for the exacting Chef Ma?"

"I actually don't report directly to him. I report to the CFO. However, whenever I attend a meeting with him, he is very down to earth. It's a great company to work for."

"I would have never guessed that you worked with numbers all day. You have a lot of sides to you. Tonight has been unexpected, but I've enjoyed it..." The way he looked at her as he said it had butterflies taking flight in her stomach.

"Oh," was all she could mutter.

"Yeah, oh." Isaac moved so quickly she didn't realise that he had pulled her chair closer until she felt her face cupped in his large, calloused hands. The way his eyes blazed with passion had her unable to keep eye contact.

"Look at me Vee."

When she did, it was in time to see him leaning in. She never would have imagined the man in front of her was capable of such tenderness. But he was. The way he gently captured her mouth, delicately sucking her tongue into his, had heat blossoming throughout her body. On instinct, her hands grasped his sweater. The sweetest kiss of her life went on for some time, even so, it seemed like it ended prematurely when he stopped it. Isaac placed a gentle peck to her lips, then her forehead.

"That was different," he remarked.

"Different good or bad?" She had to ask. As she needed to be sure that what she was feeling wasn't one-sided.

"Pretty damned amazing."

6

MY BLOODY VALENTINE

ISAAC

Issac wanted to pursue his attraction to her. However, he recognised the necessity to take a step back. Vee was his neighbour. Although he was certain after that kiss, once with her wouldn't be enough. He had promised never to plan a future with a woman again. So, how would this work? They couldn't mess around and then part ways never to see each other again.

Rather than overthinking it, he did the right thing. He slowly released her face. She frowned but recovered quickly. Until that moment, he was certain that he was going to tell her he was going to head home. Instead, he asked, "so, what's for dessert?"

Her smile blossomed as she rattled off the choices. *There. That was better*. Isaac was becoming addicted to her smile and the potent feeling of knowing it was because of something he did. That was probably the reason he agreed to dessert over a movie.

As she moved past him to go grab the movie, it was the most natural thing in the world to pull her to him and drop a kiss on her lips.

While she was gone, he explored her space. There were photos of a young Vee with a man and a woman he assumed were her parents. She looked a lot like the lady. A series of photos showed the woman's regression from healthy and vital to frail and thin. With each photo, Vee's smile was less bright and stopped reaching her eyes. It didn't go without notice the smile was always present. He admired that about her. Along the way Isaac had lost his. He used to be very much like her. The loss of his parents one after another, the dissolution of his marriage, then the final nail was losing his grandmother. He had always had a ready smile and a kind word. Then life had dumped on him repeatedly. In fact, he couldn't remember the last time he had smiled and laughed as much as he had tonight.

The photos told the story of her life. The next set of shots must have been from her college years. She had a healthy circle of girl-friends that celebrated life's moments together. The smile and cheer Isaac associated with her were present in all the photos.

As if they were secondary, her degrees were in a leather folder. He peeked inside and found she had a Bachelor's and a Master's degree in Finance.

Smart and beautiful.

Isaac had wondered if her name was short for something. *Of course! Venus. She would be named after the goddess of love and beauty.* It had initially gotten under his skin to have her living across the street. Now, he had quickly warmed to the idea of having his own Venus next door.

Jianke chose that moment to rub against his leg. "Hey Buddy, I can see why you are always over here."

The cat seemed to meow in response. While he sent his owner a look that read for Isaac not to mess up their good thing.

"It took me a while to find it, but I found the perfect Valentine's Day movie." She called as she walked down the stairs.

Isaac groaned inwardly at the thought of the over-the-top sappiness Vee had in store for him. The expectant smile on her face had him willing to endure it for a couple of hours.

"So what love fest are you going to subject me to?" He asked as she led the way to the den. She bent over to put in the DVD. Goodness, the woman had a sexy ass. Isaac was so focused he thought he had misheard her response.

"Did you say *It*? Like Stephen King's *It*?"

"Yes, the original. I don't want to watch the new one. They shouldn't mess with classics."

"Your idea of the perfect Valentine's Day movie, is *It*?"

"Yeah, I love blood and gore for Valentine's Day."

"I'm starting to think you are nothing like I thought you were."

"Or maybe I am exactly what you thought I was and more." Vee winked at him as he pulled her down and she landed in his lap, sitting sideways.

Isaac knew the moment she registered his hardness greeting her ass. Rather than shy away from it, she adjusted herself, grinding into him. The low growl was the only warning she received before he seized control of her mouth in a soul searing kiss.

The things this woman did to him. His tongue swept her mouth, demanding control. One hand gripped her waist, while the other grasped her nape. Vee matched his passion, gripping his shoulders. Isaac wanted more, but the way she was sitting on his lap hampered the access he desperately needed. He broke the kiss and took a moment to pull back to assess her.

"That was wow..." Vee trailed off. "Did you want me to start the movie?"

"The movie isn't on my current list of must haves."

"What is on your list?" Vee pressed her hand to his chest. He was certain she could feel the way it galloped under her palm.

"You. You are on my list." Issac removed her hand then placed a kiss on her palm. "I would love the opportunity to make you feel good. How does that sound?"

Her reply was to nod her head.

"Then stand for me and take me to your room." Isaac heard the demand and need in his own voice. It wasn't a side of himself he typically showed his sexual partners. He couldn't explain why he felt comfortable with Vee, like he could be himself. Without hesitancy she did exactly as she was told. Taking his hand once he stood, she guided them to her room.

Once Isaac stepped into her bedroom, Jianke appeared.

"Yeah, hell no," he said closing the door in the poor cat's face.

"You didn't have to do poor Monsieur Chat like that," Vee laughed. Although her laughter died on her lips when he turned towards her.

"Come here, Angel." She hadn't moved that far into the room, but he didn't trust his legs. He couldn't remember the last time he wanted someone as badly as he did her. She acquiesced, never taking her eyes off his. As soon as she was within arm's length, he pulled her in.

7

TRUST ME VENUS

VEE

This hadn't been how Vee had expected her night to go. Neverthe-less, there wasn't any place that she would rather be at the moment. It felt right being in Isaac's arms. His strength was an aphrodisiac that had her folds slickening.

The man continued to surprise her at every turn. When she reached him, he didn't consume her like his eyes promised. Instead, he pulled her close and nuzzled her neck.

"You smell incredible. And your skin. How is it so damn soft?" He groaned as he stroked her back. As the nuzzling turned into a sharp nip, she yelped in shock. She quickly pulled away; her eyes widened with surprise. He looked at her, a mischievous twinkle in his eye, and let out a small chuckle.

Isaac cupped her face and tilted her head slightly back. As opposed to her expectation of a passionate kiss like her last one, she received a sweet, slow kiss. The sweetness left her feeling a sense of tenderness and intimacy, as their lips gently brushed against each other, savoring the moment.

The intensity of the kiss shifted gears, and it felt like he was possessing her as he sucked her tongue deep into his mouth. He grabbed her ass as he pulled her even closer. She felt the evidence of his excitement pressing against her midsection.

Vee was so caught up in the moment, she hadn't noticed that he slid her dress up, until cool air tickled her cheeks. He traced the line of the thong, then plucked it.

Isaac ended the kiss, and spoke into her ear, "Let's get these off. You won't be needing them."

No one had ever undressed her with such sensuality. His hands were gentle, and his eyes were full of hunger. She felt her heart flutter and her pulse quicken as he removed her lingerie, exploring her body with his lips and fingertips. The way he praised her made Vee feel desired and wanted. It was a thrilling feeling that the handsome man looked at her like she was a treasure. One he intended to devour. That wasn't speculation on her part. No, he told her of his plans in explicit detail. "I'm going to take my time tasting you. My goal is to savor every moment, lick by lick. I want to experience you in every way possible."

Issac's words were so potent she could practically feel the swipe of his tongue against her slick folds. She pressed her legs together, but that only aided in the sensation strumming at her apex.

By the time she was laid naked on her bed, Vee wanted to feel Isaac moving inside her. As she watched the fine specimen undress, that desire only grew stronger. Isaac was all tattoos and defined muscles. She had never seen such a pronounced six-pack and Adonis belt in real life. How he managed that while also being beefy was a mystery. Even the veins in his lower abdomen stood out. Her mouth watered at the thought of licking them. She purred at the thought.

Everything was going well until the big reveal. Instinctively she slammed her legs together. She appreciated length, even some girth. Of course, Vee understood human anatomy. She could accommodate that wrecking ball between his thighs. But to what cost to her delicate channel? As if reading her thoughts, he joined her on the bed.

"You are looking a little worried there, Angel. Don't be. I promise to make this good for you." While he spoke, he eased his hand between her thighs. Gently stroking her folds.

"Trust me Venus. I've got you." It was phrased as a statement, but he stilled, waiting for her consent. Her nod wasn't enough.

"Tell me you want this. Me..." Pausing, he took her hand and wrapped it around his thick, hard length. Then he continued, "...as much as I want you."

"Yes, I want this." she understood that she was making a promise to trust him.

Vee allowed herself to be lost in the sensation of Isaac kissing his way down her body. He kissed her tenderly, letting his lips gently brush her collarbone. She felt a shiver run down her spine as his lips moved lower, leaving a trail of kisses on her neck. Issac tested the fullness of her globes in his hands. He suckled one diamond hard tip into his mouth, followed by the other. His tongue danced around the nipple as her core clinched in anticipation. Once he was done lavishing attention to her breasts, he languidly continued his exploration. Pressing tender kisses to her fleshy middle. When he reached the juncture between her thighs, he skipped it altogether. Her moan of frustration caused him to chuckle. As Isaac moved to her ankle, he kissed his way up to her knee and switched legs, starting back at the ankle, then moving upwards. This time, mercifully, he stopped when he reached her treasure.

The nips he delivered to her folds simultaneously ignited a heat and caused her to shiver. The first feather light lick to her nether lips had her core weeping in anticipation. For once in her life, she was completely in the moment. Every thought was hyper-focused on the pleasure the man between her thighs dispensed with aching care. Paying attention to her every reaction. It was exhilarating being pleasured with such attention. He knew how far to push the waves that threatened to wash over her without allowing her to reach her peak. It seemed to go on until she was in a state of delirium.

Muttering his name, begging him to both stop and continue. When she was certain she couldn't abide anymore, he added one, then two digits to her tight channel. With a few moves, he located her spongy spot, which set off fireworks behind her eyelids. Her breath caught as she sighed his name.

Her core clung to his fingers to prevent their retreat. Vee missed the feeling of fullness in her core. However, before she could offer a word of protest, she felt his bulbous head at her entrance.

"Look at me Angel," he demanded. His voice was low and gruff with need. Vee was rewarded with a tender smile when she complied.

"Relax for me." It was the only warning she was given as he glided his thickness into her core. The stretch stung just a bit, but he pushed forward until her walls welcomed as much of him as she could take. His rhythmic movements made her grip the sheet with one hand while the other held firm to his sculpted ass. She felt her body rising to meet his, her breathing becoming ragged as their passion intensified. His fingers gently teased her pebbled nipple as her core squeezed his length.

"So good," he praised. "Ahh, so tight," Issac stilled, then stroked his shaft within her. His movements were slow and deliberate, sending a shiver of pleasure through her body. She gasped in pleasure as he continued his gentle rhythm. *God!* Her walls squeezed him and the feeling of fullness in her core overwhelmed her. She was so close, but he was relentless as he stroked deep within. Pushing her towards the edge.

"Come for me," Issac commanded.

It wasn't the norm for her coming back-to-back. She was about to tell him just that, when her release slammed into her body, causing it to jackknife. The stream of pleasure had her singing his name. He followed immediately after, as the hot streams of his release filled her core.

Pulling out, he collapsed beside her and drew her into his arms. She listened to the thundering of his heartbeat. Exhausted and satiated, she snuggled into him.

"You're absolutely perfect, Angel." Isaac kissed her temple. She drifted off to sleep with a smile on her face.

Vee came awake suddenly to a dark room, snuggled beneath her covers. She smiled at the soreness in her core. Reaching across the bed, she found that she was alone.

8

YOU HAVE ANOTHER ONE OF THOSE SEXY DRESSES?

ISAAC

Leaving the warmth of her side was the last thing Isaac wanted to do, but he had a busy day ahead of him. Looking out her bedroom window, he assessed the snowfall. He worked out how to best serve the clients he had.

Although his back was to her, he sensed the moment she woke up. The light from outside was enough for him to observe her as he turned around. He watched as she smiled and stretched, then reached for him. That place deep inside of him reacted at seeing her frown.

Isaac had tried hard to stay away from the pull he felt toward her. His belief was that she would be too warm and cheery for him. He felt that he could not handle her enthusiasm and energy. One night in her presence changed his stance. Vee would be worth the effort. Despite his initial assessment of her, she was in fact much more complex than he had recognized. There is much more to Vee than festivities and decorations. So far, he was intrigued by what he had learned. Things were about to change for him...

"Morning Angel, I'm here," he called out to soothe her agitation.

Vee flicked on the light. Her relief was apparent as she greeted him. "Oh. Morning Isaac. I thought you had left."

Based on their previous interactions, he understood why she reached that conclusion. However, it still stung. He was also able to recognize that her feelings were valid and that he needed to take steps to address them.

"No, I wouldn't have taken off without letting you know." Walking over, he took a seat beside her on the bed, reached over, cupped her face, and gave her a peck on her lips. Issac regretted he had to take off and couldn't spend more time exploring her. She had drifted off to sleep as soon as they had finished making love. Sleep hadn't come so quickly for him. He watched her while she slept. He lay next to her, content to just take in her beauty.

"What time is it?" Vee inquired.

He looked at his watch, confirming the time. "It's three thirty."

"Why are we up?" She yawned.

"I'm up because I have to head out and start working. You go back to sleep." He adjusted her comforter, effectively tucking her in.

"Did it stop snowing?"

"Yes, it finally did. So, the guys and I will have a busy morning doing the rounds, digging everyone out. I'll make sure I take care of your property in about an hour or two."

"Thank you," she smiled. Vee really was a beautiful woman.

A plan immediately formed. "What's your day looking like?"

"I have to be at the office at nine, then I get off at five. Then just relaxing."

"Good. You are free. I will be here at seven to take you out to dinner." It had been a while since Issac was interested enough in a woman to pursue her. He almost forgot how intense he could get when he was in chase mode. He probably should soften his tone. "I just want to take you on a proper date and go from there. You good with that?"

It took longer than he would have liked for her to respond, but when she finally said, "yes, I am." He let out a breath that he didn't know he had been holding.

"Are you sure Isaac? Because I got the impression I get under your skin."

"You absolutely do. Get under my skin. But I've discovered I like you there. I have no doubt you and I will work through it all."

The scratching at the door alerted him to Jianke being up and about.

"Shit! I forgot all about my cat. He probably pissed all over your place. Listen, any mess he made, I promise to take care of it."

Vee wrinkled her nose as a fleeting expression of guilt passed over her features. "About that. Since he spent so much time visiting, I got a litter box. I couldn't take any chances."

Issac chuckled. "Now that was a wise decision. Beauty and brains. I can live with." He winked at her and placed a lingering kiss on her lips. "I will see you at seven, Angel. You have another one of those sexy dresses?"

"I will see what I can come up with. I'll walk you out."

"No, it's okay. You stay put." With a parting kiss on her forehead, he walked over and opened her door. Jianke hissed at him, jumped up on the bed, and situated himself on the pillow beside her. Where Isaac would have loved to be.

They would undoubtedly have a lot to work through. In many ways they were as different as night and day. The past, their living situation, were all reasons he should avoid pursuing this woman. Yet, the pull that he had successfully ignored the last eight months was now too strong to ignore. Vee had opened his heart to pursuing a relationship. As he did with everything, he swore then and there to give it his all.

Issac's day was more hectic than usual. He and his crew had to clear snow for his regular customers, as well as deal with a surge of clients in need of emergency help. Although he appreciated the additional business, he was exhausted from the extra work. However, he was still looking forward to taking Vee out for dinner. Unfortunately, his day ran longer than he thought it would. Issac could have kicked himself. He didn't have her number. If he drove over to her house, he could tell her he needed to change their date to a later time, which would cost him more time. Or he could call Mrs. Emmerson and ask for Vee's number. Which would no doubt start tongues wagging. Honestly, neither option appealed to him. He was in between jobs, so his truck was parked in a coffee shop parking lot. Just as he was about to place the call to his neighbour, his business phone rang.

"Hey, Issac. It's Vee." Well, this was a pleasant surprise.

"Hey Vee, I was just thinking of you."

"Well, isn't that nice? It was nice, wasn't it?"

"Yes, of course."

"I hope you don't mind me reaching out to you on your business line, but I didn't have your personal number." While she spoke, he rectified the issue.

"You have it now. I just texted you."

"Oh thanks. I'm guessing today has been a crazy day for you. My job recommended we work from home. I just wanted to offer to reschedule."

Vee just won so many points with Issac because she was so thoughtful.

This made him want to see her even more. So, Issac offered, "Or we can push it back an hour."

"Hm." she mused, then fell silent. "Okay, but how about you come over to my place for dinner?"

It wasn't a bad idea. While he wanted to be in her company. He was happy to skip going out to eat. However, he wanted to leave no question that this was a date. "Counteroffer. I come over to your place and I bring over some takeout?"

"Yeah. I would like that. Bring Monsieur Chat something to eat too."

Issac smiled as he disconnected the call. He had a feeling tonight would be the first date of many.

9

DOMESTIC VIBES

VEE

Vee wasn't able to fall back to sleep after Issac left. However, she did lounge in her bed, getting the best cat cuddles in the world. Her alarm was just about to go off when she received a message from her boss, Ramsey.

> Ramsey: Vee Lass, no need to come into the office today. The weather is piss poor, go on and take the day off.

A day off was just what the doctor ordered. It would give her time to relax and get ready for her date. After laying idly in bed, she finally got up around eight. It was nice to have a long soak after her previous night's activities. Vee finally got downstairs around nine. There was a smorgasbord of food in her fridge. She was feeling ravenous, so made herself a plate with different selections. While she ate, she put on the news.

Once they had announced they received twice the amount of snow expected, Vee wondered if she should kiss her date goodbye. She stewed in disappointment for a while. Last night had been so unexpected. One surprise after the next. Issac being the biggest of them. In one night, he had gone from being aloof to an attentive lover.

Thankfully, she was alone, so no one was around to witness her squeal. Now that they had connected, Vee could freely admit the reason it had bothered her so much that he didn't want to have anything to do with her was because she found him so attractive. Well now, they had moved past the stage of him not wanting to have anything to do with her. The rapid escalation of things would not draw a complaint from her.

Vee spent the day packaging the abundance of leftovers. Some she froze. While others she delivered to her neighbours. She saved Mrs. Emmerson for last, knowing she would be the chattiest.

"I'm so sorry I couldn't make it over to your house last night. You are the sweetest things to bring these treats over."

"It is my pleasure."

"Now I know he can be a crank puss sometimes, but on days like today, Issac could do with a package like this." Mrs. Emmerson held the bag up. "He will be out there for hours working." The woman didn't possess a subtle bone in her entire body.

Vee didn't... wouldn't add anything to the conversation. So, she smiled and wished her neighbour a good afternoon. However, Mrs. Emerson got her to wondering if Issac would make it back in time for them to go out. Maybe he would, but would he still be up for their first date? Eventually, she realized she was being selfish. Even if Issac could make it back in time, she was certain he had a gruelling day. They hadn't exchanged numbers, but Mrs. Emmerson had given her his business card long ago.

After hesitating to contact him, she called to cancel… no, hopefully reschedule their date. Vee was glad that he didn't take the easy way out of spending time with her. She had found herself cheesing by the time their call disconnected.

Maybe this was better? A nice intimate evening in. She had promised him a sexy dress. Just because they were going to remain at her house was no reason she couldn't deliver.

Later, when Vee opened the door to a punctual Issac, he wasn't smiling, but he wasn't presenting the customary frown she had become used to. However, she was certain her dress selection was the correct one. He stood at her doorway, giving her a very appreciative inspection.

"Hello Venus, I'm here for our date."

Vee gestured him in and as he passed her, he pressed a peck to her cheek. She had been concerned that the spirit of a date might be lost once they switched the venue to her home. Not only because of his declaration, but it seemed they were off to a superb start. The giddiness from earlier returned. Externally, she worked to play it cool. She offered to take his coat. He removed his boots, then placed the bags he was carrying on the floor. She was curious about the contents, but became distracted when Monsieur Chat arrived to greet his owner. The entire scene was reminiscent of a domestic arrangement rather than a date.

"What's up, Jianke?" Issac greeted, giving the cat a scratch behind his ears. The feline purred, then circled the bags. "Don't worry, your food is in one of those bags." Turning to her, he inquired. "Has he stayed in doors with you the whole time?"

Huge domestic vibes.

"Yeah, I gave him a couple of opportunities, but he looked at me like I was an insane human."

Goodness, the man had an amazing smile. "Jianke might have had the right idea about staying indoors. It was crazy out there today." Taking in his attire, she noticed he had taken the time to shower and change. There was evidence of his hair still being damp. He wore a blue dress shirt tucked into black jeans.

Once she had his coat put away, Issac picked up his bags. "Lead the way." He announced. She led him to her kitchen. "Is it okay if I place these bags on the counter?" His thoughtfulness was appreciated.

"Yes, sure." Vee couldn't wait any longer. Her curiosity finally got the better of her. "What do you have there?"

"I have dinner. I hope Italian is okay." He took out a large paper bag. She nodded. It was one of her favourites. "This is from a little mom and pop shop." As he unpacked, he informed her of the bag's contents. "We have lasagna, penne rose with roasted chicken and, of course, garlic bread."

"Sounds delicious."

"And it's still hot." From another bag, he pulled out a bottle of red wine. "For our feline friend, I have his food."

Vee took the cat's food and placed it in a glass dish. She turned to see a small African violet sitting on her counter. Her eyes were rooted to it. Pressing her hand to her chest, she bit her bottom lip, doing her damnedest to keep the tears at bay. Issac walked over to her, squeezing her arm. "Sorry, it was short notice. It's the best I could locate in a pinch."

"Oh, it's beautiful. It was my Mom's favourite plant. She loved plants. It is the one tradition of hers. I never admitted to upkeep."

He furrowed his brow and offered. "I can take it away."

"Oh no, I have the worst green thumb when it comes to indoor plants, but it really is beautiful. I will do my best to keep it alive and well."

"Then we'll work to preserve its life."

"Thank you. It really was sweet of you."

Issac pulled her into his embrace. "You're welcome." They stayed like that for a moment, but an impatient Monsieur Chat wedged himself between their feet and yowled for good measure.

"I take it he's ready to eat," Isaac groused.

They ate dinner like a couple who had done it many times before. It was as natural for her to serve him as it was for him to serve her. So, they worked together to serve each other a bit of everything. Issac told her about his day. It was very labour intensive, even though he owned the company. "I'm not one of those guys who can sit behind a desk when there is so much work to be done. The truth is, I prefer to be out in the field working."

"Did you always know you wanted to do landscaping and snow removal?" Vee was a naturally curious person, and he fascinated her.

"No, this career path is my second bite at the apple."

"What did you do before?"

"In another life, I was a police officer."

Well, that wasn't what she expected to hear. "Wow, so how did you go from being a cop to running your own landscaping business?"

"My ex found it difficult being married to a cop. The danger... it wasn't appealing to her. So, after years of soul searching, I walked away from the force." He'd loved her enough to give up his profession for her. What must that be like to have a man so devoted to you?

"If you walked away, why aren't you together?" She wondered aloud.

"All I ever wanted to do was be a cop. After I quit, I felt restless. I started helping some neighbours, then parlayed that into a business. That business required a lot of time and effort. It was too much for her. I guess I wasn't willing to sacrifice anymore. So, things fell apart." Even though he recounted the events matter-of-factly, his hurt was still evident. It was a heavy topic. However, she appreciated his candour.

"So, did you enjoy your snow day?" Issac asked probably to lighten the mood.

"I did. It was nice to take it easy. Although, I probably should have taken down the decorations outside."

"I can help you with that tomorrow." He offered. Maybe a little too eagerly for her liking. She agreed but didn't dwell on it. It left her to wonder, even though they obviously had chemistry, would such a large part of her personality be a problem for him?

10

NAPS ARE IMPORTANT

ISSAC

Issac came to with Vee pressed to his side. It took him a moment to figure out where he was. They were in Venus' living room cuddled up on her couch. After dessert, they had finally gotten around to putting on *It*. Obviously he hadn't made it through the movie. The day after a storm was always a long gruelling one, and yesterday was even more so. All the emergency clients had tipped the scale. He'd never been one of those bosses to sit behind the desk while his guys were out there working. So, he had been exhausted but hadn't wanted to break his promise to her. Not only for her sake, but he was eager to spend time with her.

The night hadn't ended as Issac had planned. Instead, he had fallen asleep on her. His watch showed it was one-thirty. He wasn't sure what his next move should be. They could stay as they were, or he could leave and go home, or they could head upstairs to her room. Either of the last two options would require that he wake her up. He glanced down at her. Venus looked so peaceful with her head pressed to his chest. He didn't want to disturb her. There was a blanket at the edge of the couch. Perhaps he could reach it without waking her up. Her steady breathing changed the moment he reached for it. He stayed still, but she slowly lifted her head, gifting him with a sleepy smile.

"You're up." She yawned, sitting up completely. He immediately missed the feel of her warmth.

"Yes, I'm sorry I fell asleep on you."

"It's okay. I know it was a crazy busy day for you."

Awkward silence filled the air. He was mesmerised by her nibbling her bottom lip. *What happens next?* Issac wasn't one to be indecisive. So, he laid out their options. "I can head out if you would like, or we can head upstairs."

"I'm good with us heading upstairs." She stood and stretched out her hand to him. Standing, he took it. The silence that accompanied them up the stairs wasn't awkward at all. Instead, it was laced with anticipation. He'd wanted to get his hands on her again since he left her bedroom. Now, as they headed upstairs, he felt energized after his nap. Issac also had time; he had a late start this morning.

Once they entered her bedroom, he closed the door behind him and stalked her to the bed. She squeaked when instead of her falling backwards onto the bed, Issac pulled her flush against his body. It felt good to have her abundant curves pressed against him. Her pillowy lips were so inviting.

A sense of connection enveloped Isaac as their lips touched. He felt like all kinds of a fool for denying them this passion for so long. In one day's span he had gone from refusing to even look in her direction to wanting more of her. He loved kissing her. The taste, smell, and feel of her seemed to be engineered with him in mind. Never being one to be neglectful of his things. His goal was to show his appreciation. Issac wanted her to feel what he felt. The need pulsing through his veins. He broke their kiss while disrobing her. Once his task was complete, Issac stepped back to admire her body. She was breathtaking. "Lay down for me Angel." The instruction made his voice gruff with anticipation. His mouth practically watered with the eagerness of tasting her.

Venus did exactly as she was told. It made him wonder how far she would go to follow his instructions. So, he gave her a few more directions.

"Spread your legs for me. I want to see." He was rewarded with her compliance. "Now touch yourself." Again, his Angel did his bidding.

Issac was mesmerized as her delicate fingers traced her slick folds. He growled when she took his instructions too far. One of her digits disappeared between her nether lips. He'd never undressed so quickly. Pulling her hand away from her centre, he brought her wet finger to his mouth. She whimpered as he suckled her essence from her digit. The sound shot straight through him. Gentleness was not the order of the day as he positioned himself between her thighs, desperate to gather more of her sweet ambrosia from the source.

At the first swipe of his tongue, his cock jumped as her tangy citrus taste short circuited his senses. Spreading her legs further, he pierced her core with his tongue. Talk about a delicious overload. As his tongue repeatedly thrust inside her, his nose stimulated her slick pearl. Her moans fuelled his desire to bring her release. Issac was relentless in his pursuit. When he tasted the telltale change of her nectar, he doubled his efforts. The reward was an immersive combination of her guttural high-pitched praise, combined with his tongue being flooded with her essence, the painful tugging at the root of his hair, and finally the clamping of her thighs around his head held him captive. Her walls and clit pulsed in unison. It was one of, if not the hottest, moments of his life.

Issac remained as he was for some time until Venus' fingers released his hair, followed by her thighs falling open. "Sorry, about... that."

"There is nothing to be sorry for." Issac dismissed her apology. He wasn't sure what she was apologizing for because all his focus was concentrated on slipping inside her warmth. He groaned in satisfaction as his leaking head breached her introitus and the warmth of her tight walls welcomed him.

"So, fucking tight Angel." He bit out. Being inside her and staying still while she adjusted to his girth was a lesson in patience. Which did not last very long. His usual deliberate strokes were nowhere to be found. Not with the sensation of her sheath gripping him so tightly. Certainly not with what sounded like a mix of her purring and moaning. No. His strokes were erratic. Gentle one moment, brutish the next. Slow like molasses, then freight train quick. He gasped along with her, as his movements caught them both off guard. His absolute undoing was her nails sinking into his buttocks. His orgasm slammed into him with such ferocity, it felt like all his senses went offline for a moment before jolting back into him like lightening repeatedly hitting the same spot. Their eyes locked as he realised her walls were spasming around him. She had found her release as well. As he was coming down off his high, he was glad of it.

Venus sighed softly, then gave him a shy smile. Issac meant for it to be a tender peck to those lips, but it turned into a tender kiss. A kiss somehow far more intimate than what they had shared. What a breath of fresh air to feel something so real, authentic... so organic.

Later, once they were all cleaned up, and she lay on his chest. Issac felt a sense of resolve. He wasn't sure how they would make it work. What he was certain of was for the first time in a very long time, he wanted to give being in a relationship a try.

11

I LIKE THE VIEW

VEE

It had taken them ten days before they could go on their first official date. Mother nature was determined to share as much snow as she could. However, during that period, they spent a lot of time together. Vee found she really enjoyed spending time with him. They shared meals together, watched murder mysteries, and had lots of amazing sex. Vee had gone her entire life without having shower sex. Now that she'd experienced it, she considered it a damn shame.

Although they were so different, she was surprised to find that they shared similarities. Most importantly, she felt like she could be herself around him. It was always expected of her to be bubbly and outgoing. She didn't have to be 'on' all the time with him.

In the beginning, she had thought he would be weary of their neighbours in the cul-de-sac learning they were spending time together. Issac didn't attempt to hide the fact that the nature of their relationship had changed. She had mentioned it to him in passing. He shrugged it off. "We have nothing to hide. We are adults. Besides, we have given them something to talk about."

Of course, she couldn't pass up the chance to sing *Let's Give Them Something to Talk About*. He'd watch her belting it out. She had offered him the serving spoon she was washing as his mic. He had taken away the makeshift microphone and kissed her soundly. Mercy, that man could kiss. It made her feel like nothing else existed. It should have been a scary experience, but she found it exhilarating.

Issac picked her up for their date. He drove into her driveway. In a car she didn't even know he owned. She wasn't surprised to see it was a muscle car. It suited him. From the moment she opened the front door, he demonstrated to her that chivalry was very much alive and well. He took the scenic route to the restaurant. All the snow was beautiful. Especially along the waterfront. The walk from the parking lot to the restaurant was short, but the wind was cold. He'd offered to drop her off to spare her, but she'd declined. Besides, she liked the way he used his body to shelter her from the gusty, frosty wind.

It was a nice restaurant but like the man, there was nothing ostentatious about it. Her ex always insisted that he order for her. Issac had no such compulsion. He did freely admit that he'd never been to the restaurant before. She liked the idea they were experiencing it together for the first time. They discussed what items on the menu looked good. "Let's just get a few things and try them out."

Issac cleaned up so well. His dress shirt fit him to perfection. "You're staring." He smirked.

"Well, I like the view." She countered.

"I doubt you are enjoying your view as much as I'm enjoying mine." Oh, Issac had game. Of course, it didn't mean he wasn't being honest. Vee did look good. She wore a fitted charcoal-coloured knit dress that hugged her curves. The V-neck plunged low. Showcasing her assets.

A gentleman stopped at the table as he was passing by. "Hey, Issac." He greeted.

"Hey Raj."

They didn't speak for long. The conversation was decidedly one-sided. Issac only nodded. Then sent him off with a mumbled, "good night."

"You seemed ecstatic to catch up with him."

Issac gave an uncharacteristic bark of laughter. "Yeah. Hardly. He, along with the rest of our pretentious neighbours were the things I was happy to lose in the divorce."

It was Vee's turn to laugh. He had a colourful way of describing things. During dinner, thoughts of the encounter were forgotten. Their meal was enjoyable, and she liked the informal way they shared the entrees. Yet another first for her.

"You were such a gentleman when you came to my doorstep to pick me up." She mused as they drove home. "Will you continue to be a gentleman and drop me off at my front door?"

Vee could hear the laughter in his voice. "I don't think anyone will accuse me of being a gentleman based on what I have planned for you."

Her body was primed to react to him. He merely suggested his plan to engage in carnal knowledge, and her core pulsed in anticipation. Vee rested her hand on his thigh, then rubbed it along its length. She felt him tense beneath her touch. Her hand migrated upwards, brushing against his growing package. Rather than say anything, he made a growling sound. The growl wasn't the only sign her teasing affected him. He abandoned the speed limit.

When they arrived at her home, they power walked to her front door. Venus barely had her shoes and coat off when she was swung over his shoulder. She squealed in delight. Damn, he was strong. Issac's steps were speedy as he moved her from the entranceway up to her bedroom. She bounced as he deposited her on the bed. By the time she sat up, he had already begun to undress. Most of his buttons were undone exposing his chest and abs. His body was a work of art that she would never tire of admiring. She couldn't look away as he discarded his shirt and unbuckled his pants.

Issac was a dominant lover, and she embraced that quality. Especially since it brought her such pleasure. However, as he freed his cock, she realised she hadn't had that bad boy in her mouth. Vee aimed to rectify that. Getting off the bed, she walked over to where he stood and sank to her knees. Still looking up at him, she stroked his length.

Her mouth watered in anticipation as a translucent beaded pearl escaped. Vee was feeling bold. No tentative licks for her. She engulfed his head in her mouth and sighed in satisfaction. Giving head was a secret superpower she had. She'd always enjoyed it. It was a sensual and erotic experience to have him in her mouth while he groaned in appreciation. She sucked on his length slowly and methodically. Until his hand grasped the nape of her neck. It was such a turn on that he was reacting to her with such passion.

"Fuck, Angel." He groaned as he guided her movements. She could taste him. He was close. However, he didn't release into her mouth.

She pouted as he pulled away. "I wanted to taste you." She pouted.

"Not now. I need to be inside you." He demanded as he helped her to her feet. Before she even realized what was happening, her dress had been hiked up, nylons and panties thrown aside. She felt herself being pulled close, his lips searing her skin as he ravaged her with passionate kisses. Then he was pushing her onto the bed and guiding himself inside of her, her moans of pleasure echoing in the room. His thrusts grew faster and more intense as he kissed her neck and whispered in her ear. Her body moved in sync with his rhythm, murmuring moans of pleasure. With every thrust, she felt herself reaching the edge of ecstasy. She gasped and her body trembled with pleasure. The feeling of bliss radiating through her body was palpable. Her breathing became laboured and her heart raced as he continued his assault on her senses. She felt her body tense and a wave of pleasure course through her as she came. He collapsed on top of her, his breathing heavy as he caught his own breath. They lay there, their bodies intertwined, content in the moment.

As she drifted off to sleep, her last thought was how right it felt being with him. It had never occurred to her that she could have a better rapport with her grumpy neighbour than anyone else.

12

CHARMING

ISSAC

The last few weeks had been great. Vee, becoming a part of his life, had been unexpected, but he felt good about it. His office manager had been the first to mention, "you seem happier lately." He couldn't deny it. She improved his mood. He tapped into a part of himself that he had closed off. The divorce had made him cynical. Now, he was feeling more like himself before his world was disrupted.

Things were looking up. There was the little matter of Nancy stopping by his office a couple of weeks back. He wasn't there when his ex-wife stopped by. Which he was grateful for. Issac had no desire to see her. The woman had a way of bringing out the worse in him. He was content to leave her in the past. Where she belonged. He didn't give her a second thought until he pulled into the parking lot of his company and saw her sitting in her car.

Issac was tempted to drive away before she could spot him, but he wouldn't allow her to scare him away from his business. He belonged here. Nancy did not. Walking past her car, he didn't acknowledge her as he opened his office. While he was making his coffee, he heard the telltale sound of a chime signalling someone had entered the front door. He steeled himself as she called out. "Hello? Issac?"

He didn't respond right away. Instead, he finished making his coffee. Then strolled out front to where she stood. "What's up?" He greeted, giving her a curt nod.

"Charming." Nancy mused as she looked around his office.

In his former life, he was a detective in the police department. So, it was a wonder to him how he couldn't tell the woman standing before him would have never been content with a life with him. Either as a police officer or as a business owner. She liked the nicer things in life. It was clear by her attire. Her coat, boots, and purse probably cost thousands of dollars. Which wasn't a problem. She could more than afford it. Her family came from money.

Nancy was a beautiful woman, and that hadn't changed. The angular bob cut of her chestnut brown hair accented her sharp features. She approached the desk, then placed her purse on it. "You have a nice place here."

"Yup." Issac nodded as he took a sip of his coffee.

She sighed in annoyance. He wasn't sure what she was expecting with her visit. "You don't have to be so hostile."

"Was there something you wanted?" The sooner he could get her out of his hair, the sooner he could get on with his day.

"I stopped by to check in. Nadia mentioned Raj ran into you. I'd meant to clear the air with you for a while." She paused and stared at him pointedly. Moving his hand in a circular motion, he encouraged her to continue. "I didn't handle the divorce well. In frustration, I acted out because being your wife had become arduous for me—"

"I'm not sure why you stopped by to bring up ancient history, but it isn't necessary. I've moved on. There is no longer a reason for your explanation."

"Hm, moved on. I heard you were on a date." Ahh, that is why she had stopped by. Nancy was fishing. Although he didn't know why, she would care. She ended things all those years ago. "I thought now that all this time had passed, you would be willing to hear my apology. Things weren't handled well. I acted out of frustration instead of talking to you." The words sounded lovely, but her snide tone belied her message. She picked up her purse. Issac hadn't needed or wanted closure, but he supposed she had given it to him. He wasn't feeling gracious enough to thank her, but it didn't mean there weren't lessons that could be learned.

Nancy returned his nod, then turned towards the exit. Stopping as she reached it, she turned back towards him. "I know you aren't great at hearing criticism, but despite what you think, I want you to move on and be happy. Make time for your new 'friend'." She used her hand to make air quotes. "It felt like you never made time for me. First, it was being a cop, and when I thought you would make time after you quit. You started a business that was even more time-consuming. I didn't mean for my visit to be a gift, but if you listen to me. It can be. Make time for her. Women really value that. Despite what you think, that's all I ever wanted from you."

Throughout the day, Issac thought about Nancy's visit and what she revealed. He wanted to dismiss what she said. After all, she had hurt him. Served him with divorce papers on his birthday. On Valentine's Day, for God's sake.

As he backed into his driveway, he looked across the street at Venus' house. Issac had come a long way from the man he was when he was with Nancy. He'd worked gruelling hours because he felt he had to. It was his responsibility to be a provider, despite what his wife had in her account. So maybe his ex's assessment was correct. He wasn't a present husband. He could learn from it, though. The gruelling hours he was working were no longer necessary to build the business. It had become a habit. One that he could ease up on.

Issac found himself rushing through his shower, so he could head over to Venus'. She was the part of his day he most looked forward to.

"Hey you're early." She greeted him as she opened the door. He gave her a quick peck, not trusting himself. At least not yet.

"I decided the paperwork could wait."

"Well. I can't complain about spending more time with you. Come in. I was just preparing dinner."

"Well, you know what they say. Two hands are better than one."

They ended up preparing dinner together. The task of peeling potatoes was assigned to him. She monitored closely. "I know I haven't had time to show you yet, but I can cook. I can handle the job."

"I can't just take your word for it. You are going to have to show me your skills." She teased.

"I think I have gone above and beyond." He wiggled his eyebrows. His playful side came out when she was around. Her laughter was addictive.

"I meant in the kitchen." She stuck her tongue out at him.

Issac put down the peeler, along with the potato. Then dried his hands on the dishcloth. He walked her back until she was trapped between the counter and him. The way she looked at him with her hooded gaze while nibbling on her bottom lip captivated him. Despite only seeing each other for a short time, he cared for her deeply.

Her thighs were parted as he lifted her to the top of the counter and stepped between them. Using his thumb, he freed her bottom lip. The kiss he pressed to her lips was gentle. He cupped her face in his hands. Yeah, it was probably too soon, but it felt right. "I think I knew I was in trouble when I met you."

"Oh, really?" Venus tilted her head. A playful smile teased her lips.

"Yeah. You mean a lot to me." Her eyes widened at his admission. "I enjoy being with you."

Her gaze dipped before returning to his. "I enjoy being with you, too."

"Good. Then we will be exclusive."

Her smile was brilliant as she nodded. Issac mirrored hers. "Dinner is going to be late." He announced before giving her a passionate kiss.

13

HEARTS AND FLOWERS

VEE

Crap. Venus wasn't expecting Issac to come back from work so early. They had exchanged keys two weeks back. Now she could hear him opening her front door. Christ, she was going to get caught red-handed. There was no way she could hide the evidence of what she was doing

"Hey Angel." He called out.

"Um, hey." Vee answered. She tried to turn over the paperwork in front of her. She jumped when he walked into her kitchen. Instead of getting up to greet him, she sat at the table like a deer in headlights. His steps faltered, and his smile died on his lips as he looked at her. Her appearance must have seemed suspicious to him. Especially with her hands spread protectively over the papers.

Normally, she wasn't a secretive person. However, she was sure he wouldn't like what she was up to. Issac stepped closer to the table.

"What do you have there?" he asked, pointing to where her hands lay.

"Um these? These are my plans for my Easter display."

Issac visibly relaxed. He took a seat beside her. "Okay... why are you guarding your plans like that?"

She exhaled. "Because of you."

"Me? I don't understand."

"I know how annoying you find my decorations. Honestly, I was thinking of scrapping the plans."

"Can I see?" He held out his hands, and she turned over the pages. As he inspected them, he whistled. "Wow. This is a lot."

"Yeah, like I said, I was just looking at them. I won't do them."

"Hey," he called gently. "Look at me. Do I think the decorations are a lot? Yes. You enjoy them, though. I don't want you to give up something you enjoy. Or change who you are. I happen to like all of you. You don't have to change a single thing about yourself. You are perfect the way you are, and you don't have to try to impress me. All I want is for you to just be who you are."

Issac had been so opposed to her decorations, she felt like she had to dull that part of her personality. Venus really enjoyed being with him. It seemed like a small sacrifice she was more than willing to make it. Even if it made her a little sad. However, she convinced herself it would be worth it. She had never felt so strongly about anyone before.

"I'm sorry if I made you feel like you couldn't be yourself." He took her hands in his and brought them to his lips. His lips brushed her knuckles. "If you need my help, I'll even lend a hand."

"You would?" Venus was genuinely surprised.

"Yeah, I think you underestimate the effect you have on me. I'd do just about anything for you." He pulled her from her chair, so she sat sideways in his lap. "I love you, Angel." Her breath caught. Vee smiled, her eyes shining with emotion. Those words caused her heart to race. A warm glow spread through her, making her heart flutter. She embraced him tightly. "I love you too, Baby."

The two of them clutched each other tightly. She felt secure in his arms. If it was anyone else besides Issac, she would have felt it was too soon. Or that they were paying each other lip service. However, he didn't say things he didn't mean. Besides, she felt it too and had for a while. Who knows how long they would have stayed locked together in each other's embrace if not for the cat?

Jianke decided he wanted to be a part of whatever was going on. He rubbed against Vee's leg. Loudly meowing, demanding to be picked up. The cat had decided both houses were his. He made his feline butt comfortable in both houses. Going and coming as he pleased. A wide variety of cat toys and treats were available at Vee's home. She picked up the cat and cuddled him. Jianke purred and rubbed himself between the both of them.

"Why are you here?" Issac inquired of the cat.

"Be nice to Monsieur Chat. I think he is our personal cupid."

"I guess so. Let's get him fed and go grab something to eat."

The following day, Issac was out meeting a new client. He'd cut his weekend hours to once a month. Now that she felt free to decorate for Easter, Vee was deep in the planning stage. Gnomes hadn't been her plan for Easter, but once she saw the Easter bunny version, they incorporated themselves into her design.

The doorbell pulled her from the world of bunnies, gnomes, and eggs. When she opened the door, there was a man on her doorstep. "Venus Desmond?"

"Yes?"

"I have a delivery for you. One moment." She tracked his movement to a flower van. The man returned with an enormous bouquet.

"This is pretty heavy. Would you like me to put it down somewhere for you?" The vase the flowers were in was ornate. It looked heavy, so she waved him inside. It was placed on her centre table at her direction. After she tipped him, then saw him out. She inspected the bouquet. There was no card. Hmm.

Vee hadn't expected Issac to send her flowers after declaring his love for her. However, it was a sweet gesture. It put a smile on her face for the rest of the day.

By the late afternoon she drifted off. She ended up taking an involuntary nap. She was awakened with a kiss to her cheek.

"Hey Angel. Good nap?" Isaac stood there smiling, holding a bouquet of white peonies mixed with light and dark pink.

"Hey, thank you. More flowers."

"More flowers?" He lifted his eyebrow.

Pointing to the bouquet across the room, she mused. "Huh. I thought you sent those."

He looked over his shoulder. "No, I didn't send those." He shook his head, then looked back to her. "No card?"

"Ah no."

"So you have no idea who sent them?" He handed his bouquet to her as he walked over to inspect the flowers.

"No. I just assumed it was you." *Hm, who sent me flowers?* Vee thought about it as she put Issac's gorgeous flowers in a vase. She should have known the other flowers didn't come from him. The bouquet was extravagant. The peonies had an understated elegance.

Issac walked up behind her and wrapped his arms around her waist. A lingering kiss was pressed to the side of her neck. "The flowers are nice."

"Hmm. Is that what you really think about it?"

"Eh. It's a lot. I'm surprised someone who really knew you sent them." Mm. Issac had a point.

"Hey, I'm going to jump in the shower before we head out to dinner." He turned her in his embrace. She felt her toes curl when he kissed her.

The shower had barely started when her doorbell rang again. Vee wasn't used to unannounced visitors. It was tempting for her not to answer, since she preferred to join Issac in the shower instead. When she answered the door, she wished to God she hadn't.

Well, the mystery of who sent the flower was solved. Her greeting died on her lips. She looked beyond the man standing on her doorstep to the front of her house. His overpriced electric vehicle was curbside.

His smile was bright as he greeted her. "Hello Venus." He leaned forward. Just as she leaned back out of reach. "Dylan. Why are you here?"

"I was thinking of you. Can I come in?"

Vee didn't want him in her home. However, she didn't want to talk to him on her doorstep where any of neighbours could view them. They hadn't seen each other in almost a year.

The last time she'd seen him had been when she ended things. He had seemed unbothered. *"I suppose it's for the best. If you intended this breakup to be an ultimatum, I'm going to have to disappoint you. I am not ready for something more official."* There could have been so much she could have said to refute his ridiculous claims. However, by the time she told him it was over, she was well and truly finished with all things Dylan Wagner. So, there was no reason for him to be on her doorstep. Vee wasn't even sure why he was at her home.

"Fine, come in." Hopefully she could get him in and out before Issac got back downstairs. She remained in the entrance.

"Can we sit and talk?"

"No. I was in the middle of something."

"Okay, fine. Did you get my flowers?" From where they stood, Issac's flowers were visible, and not the ones he sent.

"Yes, I did." She was feeling petty, so she didn't bother to thank him. "Why are you here?"

"I've been thinking about you lately. Life hasn't been the same since we split up."

Vee could practically hear her eyes rolling. *Is this guy for real?*

"It was my birthday, and it wasn't the same without your magic. Let's get married." Dylan pulled a box out of his pocket. It wasn't even a question. Just some ridiculous command.

"I'm going to stop you right there. I am not interested in being in a relationship with you, let alone getting married."

"Come on. I'm willing to give you what you want."

Vee was totally shocked. Did Dylan actually think she had been crying over him for nearly a year? She couldn't remember the last time she even thought about him. Before she could register what he was doing, Dylan closed the gap between them. He pulled her close. Gross, his mouth was all over hers.

I'm gonna knee the fuck out of him! How dare you?

"Get your fucking hands off of her." Issac commanded.

14

DON'T TOUCH WHAT IS MINE

ISSAC

Even though Isaac didn't consider himself to be a jealous guy, he hated the idea that another guy sent his woman flowers. **His woman**. In the short time they were seeing each other, Vee had him considering marriage. He'd sworn off the idea after Nancy, but his Angel changed his outlook.

Normally, he would have gone home to shower first, but he was eager to see Venus. So, he had picked up some flowers and gone straight to her house. If finding out she was sent an ornate flower arrangement got under his skin, it was nothing compared to the rage that coursed through him at finding another man kissing her. He had only been gone a short while. In that time, some man had come into her home and was kissing her. Along with the rage, was a feeling of abject hurt. So, it took him a moment to realise Vee was not at all into the kiss.

"Get your fucking hands off of her." His voice sounded decep-
tively calm, nothing like the storm raging inside. Issac ate up the
space between them and pushed the man off her. However, not
before she nailed him with a knee to the groin. The interloper
stumbled backwards, tried to right himself, but ended up landing
on his ass. Docker wearing, dress shirt sporting, preppy bastard.

"What the hell?" The other man called. "Who the hell are you?"
He demanded while trying to bring himself to his feet. "Who is he,
Vee?"

Vee was shooting daggers at the man while she wiped at her mouth
with the back of his hands. Issac hadn't seen her mad before. The
other man struggled but found his footing.

"How dare you kiss me without my permission? Get out!"

"But Vee—" the man pleaded.

"But nothing. I haven't seen you in almost a year. In that time you
thought I was sitting here pining for you? Are you insane!? L,ike I
said, Dylan, get out!! Get out of my house right now."

"Wait, let me explain." He said, uplifting his hands.

Vee marched past them and opened the door. "I swear to God. I
will call the police and have you arrested both for trespassing and
assault. Now go!"

Issac stopped himself from intervening, not only because his Angel
had it under control. But also, because he was afraid if he laid his
hand on her ex, he wouldn't be able to stop. It would be straight up
assault. It wouldn't be a good look for a former police officer to end
up in prison. Issac positioned himself, so he stood between Vee
and Dylan.

"I..." Dylan began and trailed off. When Vee shook her head vigorously, the man left in defeat. The door rattled as she slammed it behind her ex. She was so upset she was shaking.

"Come here, Angel." Issac called, pulling her into his embrace. It took more than a moment for her breathing to regulate as he rubbed her back. "Are you okay?"

"Yeah." She pulled back, and he could still see the fire blazing in her eyes.

"Let's go sit." He led her to the kitchen to have a seat. Then he poured her a glass of water. She took his hand as he sat.

"You're probably wondering what the hell that was all about."

"Yeah."

"That was my ex-partner, Dylan. We were together for five years. Once it finally got through to me that our relationship would not progress, I broke it off. I have no idea what possessed him to show up at my home almost a year later and propose to me."

"Wait what!?"

"Yeah, then he kissed me. The audacity of that man!"

"Asshole." he growled.

"Yeah. That sums him up perfectly. Getting his way is so natural for him that the idea of moving on never occurred to him. I bet you it's because he just had a birthday. While we were together, I'm the one who made sure his family, friends, and colleagues got together. It wasn't only his birthday. I kept track of the birthdays of the people in his life as well. In many ways I made his life easier."

"So, it's a case of missing a good thing once it's gone." Issac mused out loud.

"I guess you can say that."

"In that case, I almost feel bad for him." He brought her hand to his lips and pressed a kiss to her palm. "You are an incredibly special woman. I'd like to say I was sorry he didn't realise it, but then you may not be here with me."

Vee nodded and smiled. Letting go of his hand, she stood. "I have to go sanitize my mouth. Do you mind throwing out his stupid bouquet while I'm gone?"

"Sure, thing." Issac stood and pressed a kiss to her forehead.

Vee still hadn't come back downstairs after he returned from throwing the flowers into the trash bin in her garage. He found her in the closet wearing just her bra and panties. Since she was focused on the clothes in front of her, he doubted she knew he was there. She was a vision. As beautiful as she was sexy. Her curves were perfect, her skin radiant. He was a very lucky man.

"So this is where the party is?" Startled, she yelped. Then she smiled. "I guess it is."

He returned her smile, his eyes twinkling. He slowly stepped closer; his smile morphed into a predatory one. Without warning, he tugged her flush against him. He leaned in and gave her a gentle kiss. She melted against him, and their lips stayed locked for a few moments.

Issac unhooked her bra, then let it drift to the floor. She cupped him through his jeans, and all thoughts of anything else left him. He needed to be inside of her. He slid her panties off her hips, then down her legs. The scent of her arousal teased him. Spinning her around, she braced her arms on the shelf in front of her. He didn't take the time to undress, instead he unzipped his jeans and freed his hardened cock. One hand grasped her hip, while the other held his length. As his head was pressed between her slickened folds, he hissed. A grunt sounded as his lips parted, and his eyes rolled back as he pushed deeper, until he was enveloped in the warmth of her tight walls. His jaw clenched as he fought for control, his breath ragged and uneven.

He moaned as he slowly pulled out and then slammed back into her, his hips moving in a rhythmic motion. His thrusts became more intense, and the pace of his thrusts increased. "Issac," she let out a gasp of pleasure. So, fucking sexy. She tightened her grip around him, her hips rolling in rhythm with his thrusts. He teased her clit with his thumb, circling around and around. Then he traced the hooded jewel, feeling the sensitive nub underneath. She moaned in satisfaction as her hips rocked. His fingers moved faster, and she let out a loud moan. The sound shot through him. She tightened her walls around his cock. He felt the pressure build and spread throughout his body. His breathing was ragged, and his face was flushed. His movements became faster and more intense. Her essence bathed his cock, sending him over the edge. He pressed a kiss to the back of her neck.

"Let's get cleaned. Shower, then we can order in." Issac suggested.

EPILOGUE

Two years later.

VEE

Issac's truck stopped in front of the house. Great, Vee had allowed time to get away from her. Now, she had been caught red-handed.

"Hey Angel, what you doing there?" He asked as he exited his truck hastily. Yeah, he definitely wasn't a happy camper. It was apparent as his strides hastily ate up the space between them. He stopped in front of her and took the nail gun from her hand. Then reached out his hand for hers. She took it and stepped down from her small perch on the stepladder.

She partially covered her face with a hand. "I can explain."

"Yeah, please do." His stance was intimidating. He reminded her of the Issac she first met.

Allowing her hand to slip, she put some steel in her spin. She was a grown woman. "I was on the couch resting like you and the doctor told me to do."

"Ah, huh."

Issac frowned as she explained. "Then I forgot I didn't add the ballet skirt to the cupids."

"I see. Why couldn't you have waited for me to get back?"

"Because I have been a lot with getting the Valentine's Day decorations." She really had been.

"I told you I don't have a problem with that." He used his forefinger to lift her chin. "Do you know what I do have a problem with?"

Vee shook her head. "No. Don't do that. You do know. I have a problem with my very pregnant wife, who is supposed to be resting. being out here on a ladder. Are you insane?"

He placed his hand on the small of her back. "Inside." he commanded.

"You're not the boss of me." She pouted.

"The hell I'm not."

"Hey where are my snacks?" Issac had nipped out to get her garlic sauce, all dressed Ruffled chips and lemon crème cookies. It was her new craving. The perfect mixture of sweet, tangy, and salty. It was genius, really. What she did was open the lemon cookie sandwich, placed two chips in between them, then dipped the resemble cookie in garlic sauce. Just the thought of it made her want to do a little jig.

"They are in the truck. I forgot all about them when I saw you out there on a damned ladder."

"It was a stepladder." She defended.

"I don't see the difference. Go sit down. I'll get your snacks."

Vee waddled her way to the couch and had a seat. Did she really want to put her feet up? No. but he would fuss if he came in and they weren't up. It felt like she had been pregnant forever and the recent restrictions didn't help. Two weeks ago, the doctor had recommended she stop working early. Her husband had been positively gleeful. It had been over a year since they got married and it still made her smile when she thought of being his wife, or him being her husband.

The proposal had been perfect. It was also only six months after they started dating. They had been having a movie night. Issac excused himself to go get ice cream in the kitchen. Monsieur Chat had jumped up into her lap, sporting a new collar.

"Hey, you got Monsieur a new collar?" She cuddled the cat. Thankfully, it was one of those days he was down for the extra affection.

"Yeah, he was due for a new one." He answered as he came back into the room. "Take a look."

"Oh, my God!" she exclaimed when she realised that the collar had words and what they read.

"Venus Desmond, will you marry me?" When had he slipped to his knees?

"Yes!" she answered enthusiastically. Issac slipped the beautiful princess cut diamond ring on her finger. It fit perfectly. The ring

couldn't be more her if she had selected it herself. It was a testament to how well they had gotten to know each other.

The couple had agreed on a shorter engagement. They didn't need or want a large wedding. Although it wasn't large, that didn't mean it wasn't a stunning one. The ceremony was at a butterfly conservatory. The reception? Well, because of Vee being fortunate enough to work for Ma Kitchens, Chef Aaron Ma offered her the reception room at Fusion. Proving he and Ramsay were the best bosses ever, Chef Ma personally came up with the menu. Adding the cherry to an already perfect sundae. The venue, food, and drinks were a present from her employers.

"We just want to thank you for improving the company's morale with all you do." Chef Ma explained. Ramsay had taken it a step further; he had given her a week paid vacation along with a paid honeymoon. "It's been a tough year for Aaron and I. You've been ace."

They had a beautiful day. Issac wore the hell out of his tux. Vee looked at their wedding portrait on the far wall. They were a striking couple. Not only did she feel like a princess on her special day, but she looked like one, too.

Vee heard Issac come into the house, but he disappeared into the kitchen. She was still getting used to the layout of the house. They had just completed renovations four months ago. Due to the sentimental value of his house, they decided to move into Issac's. Vee's house was being rented out. Speaking of her house, that is how Vee learned her husband was pretty well off. His wedding gift to her was paying off her mortgage.

Sleep must have claimed her for a short while because when she came to, it was nearly an hour later.

"Ahh, you're up, sleepyhead." Issac commented as he rubbed her feet which had made their way into his lap. "Ready for your snack now?"

"Yes, just let me go to the washroom." Vee made the trip to the washroom and when she returned, her snacks were waiting for her. She assembled her masterpiece.

Issac shook his head at the sight. "I'm really sorry our son is making you eat that." He mused. The couple had decided they needed to know the gender of their child. Although, they were both happy just to have a healthy baby. They already picked his name and had been using it on the little guy nestled in her womb. Orion Victor Lam was due in a week. They were going to have another February birthday. Issac still wasn't big on celebrating his born day, but it wasn't the sore spot it used to be. Instead, he concentrated his efforts on making Valentine's Day special for Vee. After all, it marked the day he got his head out of his ass and claimed Venus as his own.

He had plans for Valentine's Day that were top secret. They had come a long way from him hating the day to making a special plan. It brought a smile to her face. They had come a long way from when she moved in, and he wouldn't even look in her direction. She was no longer his Venus next door. They shared a home together and were building a life.

The End

Jianke

AFTERWORD

Thank you reading Venus Next Door.

Before you go, please leave a review and I'd appreciate it if you told a friend about this book.

ACKNOWLEDGMENTS

As always, I'm grateful for my tribe.

First to my amazing husband, Mr. Z you make all this possible. Love you +

Thank you all for your encouragement, support, and guidance. You all inspire me to keep telling the stories in my head.

Thank you to my editors. You guys are beyond amazing.

The best writing partners in foreverdom, Darie & Brianna.

Especially these ladies that hold a special place in my heart: Kim(PIC), Amanda, LaJoyce, Evelyn, Samantha, Terreece, Carla, Kim L., Tee, Viv, Ava, & Leah.

To the readers, thank you for reading and providing your feedback. I appreciate you all so much. You motivate me to keep writing. xoxo

EMULSIFY: MEANT TO BE EXCERPT

If you would like to know more about Vee's boss Chef Aaron Ma and find what he went through, read about it in his book Emulsify.

Emulsify: Meant To Be (Elite Series Book 2)

Please see the excerpt below:

Prologue
Aaron
2014

Outwardly, Aaron Ma appeared calm. Unbothered even. However, inside, he was seething.

"Do you see why public personas shouldn't screw journalists?" Ramsay Russell, his business partner, asked the moment Aaron lifted his eyes from the pages of the magazine.

Who in the hell did Tori Mathers think she was?

She sure the hell wasn't a journalist. This article... No, this was not an article. It sounded like something penned by a scorned woman. A hit piece. Except she had no reason to act scorned. He had been upfront with her. Let her know from the start that he wasn't inter-ested in a relationship with her. All they could share was the physical.

"Well, I had no idea it would turn out this way. Tori was all for our agreement." Aaron finally answered Ramsay.

Tori had taken it well. Or so he thought. The moment Aaron and his fiancée announced his engagement things changed. Ten months after their agreement had ended! First had come the drunken texts and calls. Then, the barely hinged visit where she had spewed accusations as she cried and wailed.

"Oh, for me, you weren't ready for a relationship, but for that bland mousy woman, you are suddenly ready to settle down! Is it because she's young? Or is it because she's your partner's sister? What makes her good enough for a relationship and marriage but not me?" Tori had raged.

In hindsight, now that Tori had taken her vendetta public, maybe he shouldn't have been so dismissive.

"Is that what you think? I've told you repeatedly that the previous 'arrangements' you made with women would blow up in your face. All it would take was one! One crazy bitch to bite you in the ass."

Fine, so Ramsay had a point. The woman trashed him personally. Labelling him a playboy, who was only interested in his own plea-sure, ignoring the needs of his partner. *Like she had ever left his bed without coming multiple times.* So, she was full of shit, but he could let that slide.

What Tori wouldn't get away with was besmirching him professionally. Implying he wasn't worthy of the many accolades that he had accumulated. That he looked down his nose at his peers. Tori had made Aaron out to be a talentless diva that lived for fame. Nothing could be further from the truth.

Aaron had worked tirelessly to become an acclaimed chef. He was renowned worldwide because he was a master in the kitchen. He had a career that spanned over twenty years, and he wouldn't allow the likes of Tori Mathers to crumble what he had built.

Aaron would annihilate Tori the way she was trying to do him.

"Well, Tori has left me with no option. I'm going to have to sue her." Aaron shook his head and sighed heavily.

"Have you lost your mind? You are playing right into her hands." Ramsay fumed.

"I suppose you have a better idea?"

"As a matter of fact, I do."

Oh great, Ramsay was smirking. "Ramsay, why do I feel like I will not like it?"

Chapter 1
Brooke

How many rich and famous people had she encountered in her lifetime?

Many... Too many to count.

Yet, as the door to the private dining room swung open with a swish, the sight of him strolling into the space caused her breath to hitch. She brought her hand to her chest as if it could aid her in returning to regular breathing. Nice normal breaths. Not the unruly ones that were getting caught in her throat.

No amount of research could have prepared Brooke Éloissaint for her first in-person glimpse of Aaron Ma. Even though she had spent hours poring over pictures and footage of the man to prepare for the article, she was there to write.

Handsome.

Good looking.

Gorgeous.

All seemed inadequate descriptions. He was simply...beautiful. The words sexy, swag, and cocky followed that assessment. It was all there in his purposeful strides.

"Brooke..." her boss, Bartholomew, called. How had she forgotten that there were other people in the room?

Bartholomew had been off to the side speaking with Ramsay, Aaron's business partner. She hadn't realized the two men had moved closer, much closer, and now stood by her side.

"Let's get you and Aaron introduced so we can get you settled," Bart continued.

Her gaze and attention drifted to the man of the hour. Aaron Ma seemed taller than his statistics had mentioned. Perhaps his heavily muscular swimmer's build made him appear taller than the reported 6'2". He wore his inky jet-black hair pulled back off his face. More than likely, in a ponytail, the man had long, flowing hair. Its rich blackness seemed to shimmer under the lights.

Aaron reached the three and he graced them with a smile. Although it held tension, it was no less devastating. His smile was radiant, with perfect white teeth, enhanced by unexpected deep dimples embedded in each cheek.

"This is Bartholomew Hjelmstad, one of *Folks'* owners. Bart, this is Chef Aaron Ma." Ramsay introduced the men. They briefly shook hands when Aaron extended his hand. As they exchanged pleasantries, the deep timbre of Aaron's voice, married with his posh British accent, produced goosebumps along Brooke's arm.

"This is Brooke Éloissaint..." Ramsay continued. Aaron's arm stretched out toward Brooke, and his large hand engulfed hers, swallowing it up. After a moment of staring at the golden-tanned hand, Brooke looked up to find chestnut-colored orbs watching her. It was surprising, as his mono-lidded almond-shaped eyes looked much darker in all the photos.

"...she will be the journalist covering the human-interest piece on you."

His thumb that had been stroking her hand stopped mid-stroke, and only then did she register what Aaron had been doing.

"Pardon, come again?" The question was posed to Ramsay as Aaron suddenly released her hand as if it were searing his skin.

"Now, Aaron, I know this isn't exactly what we discussed."

"Correct, this is in fact, just the opposite of what we discussed. I apologize for wasting your time Bartholomew, Brooke, and that you came all the way here. This interview is not happening." Aaron announced.

Both Bartholomew and Ramsay regarded each other, eyebrows raised, jaws slack. Brooke watched as Aaron slightly inclined his head in her direction and strode off until he disappeared beyond the door he had entered the room from earlier.

"I'm sorry about this. Stay right here. I'm just going to have a chat with him and be right back. Please have a seat." He instructed as his Scottish brogue became more pronounced. For a big man, he moved swiftly until he too, disappeared out of the room.

"Aaron! Hold on, not so fast." Were the last words Brooke heard before the door swung closed.

"Bartholomew?" Brooke asked, turning to her boss. She took a seat at the long table, and he sat beside her.

Sheepishly, he answered, barely making eye contact. "I'm sorry about that."

"It seems messy, and I don't do messy. I didn't even want to do this."

"I know, and I still think you are the best person to do this piece. Let's just let Ramsay work his magic."

"And then what? It's obvious Aaron doesn't want me here."

"Aaron might have believed the journalist was male."

"Hmm, and who gave him that impression?"

"Ramsay might have felt it was best to let him believe that."

"What the hell? What did you two think would happen when he realized I obviously am not a man? Did you think of the position you were putting me in?" Brooke admonished. Although

Bartholomew was her 'employer,' the two had been friends since university. Their conversations were often free of restraint.

"I'm sorry about this, Brooke. We will make it right, and I promise I'll make it up to you."

"I think it's best we just leave well enough alone. Aaron obviously doesn't want to do this interview. Hell, I am surprised he agreed to it. I wouldn't trust *Folks*. After that article Tori was allowed to publish."

"Well, you know that shit didn't happen on my watch, Brooke. That was the catalyst for me to take the helm. I can turn the magazine around and make it what it was. I know if you work with Aaron, it will repair our image not only with him but the people we want coming to us to share their stories. I will keep my promise and give you the latitude to do more serious pieces if you do me this solid."

"Ugh. I will keep my word, but I don't think you two will get Aaron to agree to this. It seemed like he had a pretty good idea of what he wanted."

"Brooke, I have a good feeling about this. I'm sure this will work out. You'll see, this will be a great experience for all involved."

"If you say so, Bartholomew."

"Ramsay is very convincing, and he will bring Aaron around." They fell into a comfortable silence as Brooke took in their surroundings. The private dining room in which they were seated was located in Aaron Ma's flagship restaurant. Currently, reservations were fully booked for the next six months. A warm aubergine and silver colour scheme decorated the room...It was elegant and simple, a muted representation of the owner. Aaron was vibrant and bold.

Ramsay entered the room followed by Aaron, interrupting her thoughts. Neither man looked pleased, so Brooke couldn't determine which one of them had won the battle. When they both reached the table, they sat across from where Bartholomew and Brooke sat.

Ramsay finally broke the silence. "Aaron has reconsidered his stance in participating in the article."

"Excellent, you and Brooke–" Bartholomew started.

"Not so fast. First, I have some questions and some conditions before I agree to proceed." Aaron interrupted.

A feeling of apprehension settled over Brooke as Aaron's eyes moved to hers. An air of weariness blanketed his features. His firm jaw set, lightly sprinkled with a five o'clock shadow, showed his disapproval.

"How much of my time do I have to give you, Brooke?"

"I would say two to three weeks."

"What will this lengthy process involve?" Aaron asked, his voice peppered with sarcasm. Brooke bristled at his tone.

"Well, Mr. Ma—"

"If you want to be formal, it would be Chef Ma, but you can call me Aaron," he curtly interjected.

"Well, Chef Ma... Aaron," she amended as he arched one thick, shaped brow.

"I need to get to know who you are so that I can give a comprehensive portrait."

"What kind of access to my life will you require to 'get to know me'?" He asked, his voice full of challenge.

"Professional and personal. All of it." Her response matching his tone.

"There has been a lot written about me over the years, and I'm sure you can find what you need from that."

"I guess, if you want yet another superficial piece written about you, that has no depth. Why don't you just hire a publicist to give whatever narrative you want to put out there?" She challenged.

A light chuckle from Ramsay reminded Brooke that she and Aaron were not alone. He was rubbing her the wrong way, and her usually chilled, unruffled personality was nowhere to be found. Had she found him attractive moments before? Yes, but now his 'personality' erased all that work mother nature had curated. Looks could not hide that she found him boorish.

Brooke reminded herself she was a professional, and this opportunity would be the gateway article into writing more serious pieces. No, she wasn't excited about capturing the life of some celebrity chef. She had not spent all those years obtaining a master's degree in journalism and communication to only write fluff pieces.

A change in tone may help. "Aaron, I will try to be as unintrusive as I can. My role will be to observe and document your everyday life. Now, in terms of how you have gotten to where you are, it will require me to delve into your history. I will do my utmost to do it as respectfully as possible."

"I suppose I can work with that. My one condition is that I get final approval of the article before it goes to print."

"Excuse me? Repeat that again." Brooke really was asking for clarification. She couldn't possibly have heard him correctly.

"I'm certain you heard me. However, no one at your little magazine will ever have my consent to publish anything about me without my express approval."

"Nan mède." She swore under her breath. This was certainly a shit show. Well, today had been a waste of time. She wouldn't be agreeing to any such thing.

"What was that?" Aaron smirked. By the look on his face, she was certain he had heard and understood her. Who cared? At least she wouldn't have to work with him.

"Aaron, I think we can come to an agreement on that matter," Bartholomew offered.

No, the hell they could not! It took all of her energy not to whip her head in Bart's direction and glare at his ass. Instead, she took a measured breath and turned to him. Trying to force herself to sound calm, she plastered a manufactured smile on her face.

"Bartholomew, I am not sure how we could. After all, that is not how things are done. I certainly am unwilling to invest all that time into writing a piece on Chef Ma, only for him to censor me."

"I'm sure Aaron isn't looking to censor you. He doesn't know us, but I have no doubt your work will speak for itself. That he won't have resistance."

Brooke was stuck between a rock and a hard place. All eyes were now on her. Bartholomew's and Ramsay's expression begged her to play along. Whilst Aaron smirked. Practically daring her to refuse his unreasonable request. She saw it. That he had expected her to refuse. Well, she was up for the challenge.

"Sure, I can agree with that. However, to be more thorough, I will have to add a week or two to get this just right."

His burgeoning smile died on his face. *Checkmate.*

ABOUT THE AUTHOR

Award-winning authour Niccoyan Zheng is a Canadian wife and mom to an amazing little guy. She loves travelling, but you'll find her asleep en route. A lifelong reader, she loves great mysteries and epic love stories. Dubbed the 'Queen of Second Chance romances'. Niccoyan is a firm believer in letting the characters guide the story. (As if, they'd allow her not to) Her stories are rich in diversity and culture. While evoking a wide range of intense emotions.

Niccoyan Zheng's Web Site

I've loved sharing my characters with you. To find out what's next please use the QR code below to sign up for my Niccoyan Zheng's Newsletter.

ALSO BY NICCOYAN ZHENG

Consumed: A Darkish Romance

Retrograde: Forget Me Not

Cupid's Kiss: A Penning Valley Valentine's Day Anthology

Emulsify: Meant To Be (Elite Series Book 2)

Pleasurer: KNK Matchmaking Agency

Left (Kindle Vella)

Frenchie: Sin City MC Oakland Chapter

My Last Aloha, Love

Sensory Desire

www.ingramcontent.com/pod-product-compliance
Lightning Source LLC
Chambersburg PA
CBHW051303170626
46809CB00004B/1759